Lucy's Mindfu

'when lucy meets arden'

Written By
Leona McDonnell

Illustrated By
Laura Phillips

Lucy's Mindful Life
'when lucy meets arden'

Copyright 2022 © Leona McDonnell
www.leonamcdonnell.com

Creative Consultant: Caoimhe McDonnell

Published by The Book Hub Publishing Group
www.bookhubpublishing.com

ISBN: 978-1-7391012-0-6

Dedication

For my loving family Gerry, Caoimhe, Caolán and Sadhbh, our animals and Mother Earth.

You are the greatest teachers that I will ever have in my life!

For free 'when lucy meets arden' PDF workbook go to:

www.lucysmindfullife.com/workbooks/when-lucy-meets-arden.pdf

For guided 'Breathe and Root' audio meditation go to:

www.lucysmindfullife.com/audio

Chapter 1

Meet Lucy and her Family

Lucy lives in a small stone cottage in the countryside with her mum Maeve, her dad Conor and her little brother, Jack. There is always some fun, laughter and mischief going

1

on in Lucy's family. Every morning, as Lucy gets up and is preparing for school, she can hear her mum singing

♫♫ ♪

"Good morning good morning good morning"

at the top of her lungs in the kitchen. Lucy often catches her mum dancing around the kitchen table to the songs on the radio as she flaps her arms and shakes her whole body while enjoying

the fresh morning breeze blowing through the house

from all the windows and doors that are open.

Her dad Conor usually

rolls out from his bed

every morning. He slowly makes his way

up to the kitchen with his hair sticking up on his head as he rubs his eyes. One particular morning, he was so sleepy that when he walked into the kitchen, Lucy's cat Tinkerbelle jumped off the kitchen countertop, where she was stealing chicken that had just been cooked and was cooling in the pot on the cooker. She then ran across the floor in front of Lucy's dad.

He stumbled as he tried not to
fall on Tinkerbelle and he
clumsily stubbed his toe
against the kitchen table.

That fairly woke him up and as he
screeched "Ouch, you naughty cat",
he flung off his shoe. Lucy could

only giggle as she saw her dad's big toe sticking out of the top of one of his socks. There was a huge hole in his sock and when he came back up from his bedroom having gotten a new one, Lucy was laughing so hard

Ha ha! Ha ha!

at what she saw! One sock was bright pink and the other was navy with light blue polka dots. Lucy thought it was so funny and she loves how playful and funny her dad is.

Lucy's little brother Jack is one year younger than she is and he is so full of excitement and mischief. He is always playing pranks on his family like jumping out from behind the doors or from under the beds and surprising them or spreading ketchup on his legs and pretending that he has fallen and cut himself. He loves to run wild with their dogs Tilly and Sam, chasing them and tackling them to the ground to try and get the balls out of their mouths. He often locks his arms and legs around their Golden Labrador Tilly and

tumbles and rolls

down the hill beside their house as he laughs at how Tilly howls with excitement. Sam, their little Yorkshire Terrier, loves to race alongside them and to jump onto Tilly's belly as they come to a big thud at the bottom of the hill.

Jack often jumps down from a tree he's climbing in front of Lucy as she's passing by and pranks her. Lucy loves Jack and he is her very best friend but she finds that he can be really cheeky sometimes as he's always up to tricks.

Lucy and Jack's Granny and Grandad love to come and visit

them. They love to relax and enjoy spending time together outside in the countryside, in nature, going for long walks, feeding all the wild birds living in their garden and rubbing Lucy and Jack's pet pig Penny.

Sometimes, when Grandad Joe rubs Penny's belly, she throws herself down into the mucky puddle beside her pen and she lies on her back to get her belly rubbed. She snorts and

groans as she enjoys getting
scratched. Although, Granny Anne
does not think it is very funny when
Penny

kicks, and splashes

them all with dirty muck and smelly
pig water.

Lucy loves to watch Granny Anne
knitting as they sit cuddled up in a big

old armchair by the fireside under a lovely, large fluffy, red blanket. She smiles like crazy when Granny Anne teaches her how to knit. Jack loves to dig, plant, seed and mess around in the garden outside with Grandad Joe. He loves to ask Grandad Joe about the types of trees that are growing in their garden, the different types of leaves and colours that they each have but he mostly loves to listen to Grandad Joe as he tells Jack old stories of when he was a young boy and the trouble and playfulness that he used to get up to as well. Jack enjoys hearing Grandad Joe telling him of how he had to work on his own dad's farm every

day to collect and deliver the cows' milk, to feed the herds, to clean out the cattle pens and to fix anything that Granny wanted repaired around the house. Jack really wanted to be like his Grandad Joe when he got older.

Lucy really loves their animals and she has a very special connection with them. She enjoys spending time with her animal friends and she loves to cuddle, hold and pet them. She loves to watch Tilly as she playfully chases the birds flying overhead to the bird feeders hanging in their garden. She finds it so funny when Sam coughs and sneezes and jumps around as he tries to catch a little butterfly that has landed on his nose and is tickling him.

She giggles as she watches Tinkerbelle doing a

roly poly tumble

after a leaf blowing in the wind. They bring her a lot of joy and leave her with a lovely warm and cosy feeling inside of her heart and body when she plays with them.

While Jack loves making up
adventures and games to play outside,
Lucy enjoys listening to the birds as
they sing, tuning into the rustle of the
leaves swaying on the trees and to

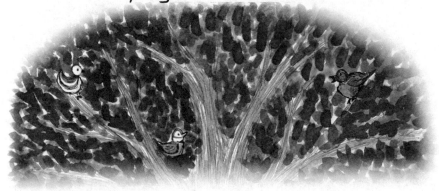

the gentle sound of the wind
blowing and whistling.

She always feels very calm, relaxed
and worry-free when she is outside
in nature.

But she often has to tell Jack to stop
making so much noise outside as he
skids around their house on his go kart,

kicking and
splashing water,
stones and mud
everywhere as he
competes in his imaginary grand prix
race. Jack is so focused on the
moment he is in as he tears up the
gravel path leading to their house that
he hasn't got time to listen to Lucy.
He is too busy making sure that he

steers all of the other competitors in the grand prix off the track and that he wins every single race!

Just like with the noise that Jack makes racing around the house on his go kart, Lucy finds that her mind can also be very noisy with loud and banging thoughts that just keep swirling around buzzing around like bees inside her head.

These can be thoughts about something that happened yesterday or thoughts about something that might happen tomorrow. She often finds it hard to concentrate and to get the buzzing bees in her mind to quieten down, so that she can just notice what she is doing in the moment she is in.

When Lucy's mind feels this busy, she finds herself getting

anxious, nervous, tired and worried.

When this happens, she can feel her heart starting to beat faster or she can notice her breathing getting quicker. Sometimes she gets a pain inside of her tummy and other times her hands and feet start to sweat. Lucy can become dizzy and her legs sometimes shake and feel weak. She doesn't like these feelings and emotions when they come to visit her and she doesn't like how they make her mind and body feel. In fact, they can make her feel quite scared. Lucy wishes that she knew how to calm down all these buzzing bees in her mind. All she wants to do is to be able to be happy and to enjoy her time outside playing and spending time in nature and with her animals, even if she has to keep telling Jack to stop making so much noise! If only Lucy could find out how to calm down her busy mind. If only she could learn how to do this for herself...

Chapter 2

Fun, Easy, Silly Sundays

The next morning, as Lucy slowly opened her eyes and stretched out her arms and legs like a big starfish, she could see the morning sun peeping in under her curtains in her bedroom. As she was

making funny hand
and bird shapes
in the shadow
of the sun shining
against the bedroom
wall, she suddenly remembered that it
was Sunday, which are always fun, silly,
easy and relaxed days in her house.
So she

jumped out of bed,

threw open her curtains and her
bedroom window and took a long
deep breath in of the fresh crispy
Autumn morning air, filling up her
lungs to the very top.

She then raced up to the kitchen to see if Jack had made it up to the TV before her as she wanted to watch her favourite weekend cartoon but as she ran into the kitchen, she was stopped in her tracks when she noticed Jack lying on the couch watching his racing programme. She looked at Jack and he smiled back at her. Something then caught her attention in the corner of her eye and she and Jack immediately started to howl with laughter!

As she stood and stared out of the kitchen patio door onto the garden, Penny was standing staring back in at her. Her nose and mouth were pressed against the glass on the door and Lucy could see Penny's slobber and drool running down the glass. Penny was in a trance watching Lucy's dad eating his breakfast and staring at the puddle of scrambled egg and toast on the floor where he was messily dropping it as he ate. Lucy smiled as she imagined Penny saying to herself

"Yum, please can I have some of your breakfast?"

But poor Penny didn't get any of dad's breakfast because Tilly swooped in past Lucy and devoured the spilled mess before Penny could even protest.

As Jack had beaten Lucy to the TV and was teasing her that she should have got out of bed earlier, Lucy decided to get her breakfast, to get dressed and go outside to help her mum feed their animals. As usual, Lucy's mum was singing at the top of her lungs and she called to Lucy to come and have a morning bounce on their trampoline. It was so

enjoyable as they both did hand bounces, knee bounces, belly bounces and bum bounces in the sunshine. They laughed so hard and Lucy felt so full of happiness.

They both sat on the rocks in their garden to catch their breath after bouncing so much and noticed how the leaves looked like they were doing a little dance as they somersaulted through the air

with the light morning breeze. They could almost see and hear the flowers giggling and laughing as they danced in the gentle breeze, the grass growing and the trees whispering.

Lucy then whispered to her mum that she thinks that the beautiful trees in her garden are full of life, fun and happiness and that they are always whispering and laughing with one another.

As she sat on the rocks with her mum, Lucy suddenly heard a noise behind them, and turned around quickly telling her mum that she had seen the old trees in her garden winking at each other and waving their branches, swaying in the breeze, just like she does when she is dancing and jumping around with joy. She then jumped up off the rocks and turned around to face these wise old trees again and she could see them smiling from ear to ear as they played 'I spy with my little eye' and 'count the flying birds'. It looked like they were having such great fun.

All of a sudden, Jack came racing around from the back of their house on his bicycle with Tilly and Sam running in full speed beside him. He was making a racing engine noise with his mouth as they all whizzed by Lucy and her mum. They could only laugh at his excitement. Lucy then made her way over to her favourite old tree in her garden and threw herself down on the ground in front of it. As soon as she reached the ground, Tilly, Sam and Tinkerbelle climbed up on her and were cuddling her with happy grins on their faces.

As she rested her back against this beautiful strong tree and its solid trunk, Lucy gently closed her eyes and was starting to let go of all the excitement she just had and enjoy this lovely moment when, all of a sudden, Jack fell headfirst down on the ground in front of Lucy. He had been hanging off a low branch in the tree over Lucy's head and he was planning to prank her once again but then he lost his grip and plummeted down at Lucy's feet. Lucy shrieked as she heard the bang but as soon as she heard Jack giggling and shouting, "fooled you" and as she saw Tilly and Sam licking him, she knew that he was alright.

Even though the morning had been full of fun, action and laughter, Lucy started to have the familiar feeling of

worry and sadness

as she knew that she had to go to school in the morning. She did like school but she found it difficult being away from her family. Lucy also felt that sometimes she didn't really 'fit in' with her classmates and she felt different. She often felt lonely and left out and she found it easier to stay by herself wishing that she could feel more confident and happier in herself when she was away from her family.

Lucy continued to rest against her favourite old tree with her animals but the buzzing bee thoughts in her mind got louder **and louder**

and her head spun quicker and quicker.

She then felt a soft teardrop drip from her eye and it gently landed on one of the big old roots of the tree. All of a sudden, she could hear a soothing voice saying, "It's ok, Lucy, it's ok to feel sad and it's ok to cry."

Suddenly, Lucy felt a beautiful feeling inside and outside of her body. She had never felt this feeling before. She felt as if she was being wrapped up in the safest, warmest, cosiest and most wonderful loving blanket. She felt as if she was melting deep into this blanket and even deeper into the earth below her as she lay against this magnificent tree. She wondered what was happening. Did she fall asleep? Was she dreaming? What was going on?

Chapter 3

Breathe and Root

Lucy felt like she was melting and drifting deeper and deeper and as if she was being cuddled by the branches of her favourite old tree. It was almost as if the tree was wrapping its strong, caring arms around her to help her to feel safe, calm and protected as her mind was racing with thoughts about going to school the next day.

Next of all, she could see the tree's beautiful wide smile. Then she heard another gentle whisper into her ear, "Hello Lucy, my name is Arden and I am your special nature friend. I have been waiting for this moment for some time. I am here to teach you how to calm those busy thoughts in your mind. I am here to help you to learn how to feel peaceful, safe and still in your mind and in your body. But for the minute,

just **breathe, Lucy,**

just **rest**

and **breathe**".

Arden then said to Lucy, "Now Lucy, I want you to put one hand on your heart and one hand on your tummy and just feel how your body moves

as you breathe in
and as you breathe out".

He continued by saying to Lucy,
"Take a breath in through your nose
and feel your tummy rising up and
filling full of air. Then, slowly breathe
out through your mouth and feel
your body releasing and letting go of
any fears, scary thoughts or
worries that you have in your mind
or body about going to school
tomorrow, being away from your
family or about anything else. Now,
feel your tummy falling and emptying

as you blow all the air out through your mouth. I would like you to stand up and drop your hands down by your sides, with your palms facing forward and I want you to imagine that you are standing tall and strong, just like me. Feel me pulling your whole body deep below the earth and using my roots to help to anchor you to the calm and peaceful earth, just like I am. This is my very special 'Breathe and Root' practice and I am so happy to share it with you. Now I want you to use your imagination and picture long, strong roots coming out from the

soles of your feet. Imagine these roots growing and spreading deep down into the ground and helping you to feel strong, solid and connected to the earth. Now, Lucy, repeat this three more times and see how you feel".

Lucy smiled happily to herself and she felt so comfortable, safe and warm as she finished the 'Breathe and Root' practice and as she sat back down against Arden. As she rested there and did another three breaths in and out, with one hand on her heart and one hand on her tummy, she could hear Jack

chasing after Penny in the distance
and she could hear Penny squealing
with delight. But Lucy was so calm
and relaxed in that moment that her
mind didn't wander off to see what
Jack and Penny were doing, it
stayed where she was while she was
doing her 'Breathe and Root'

practice
with Arden.
She could
feel her
roots being
pulled down
through her
feet and

anchored deep into the earth below her. Lucy was amazed at how peaceful, how soft and how quiet her mind and body felt now. Even Tilly, Sam and Tinkerbelle were all comfortable and peaceful. Tilly was so cosy, that she had rolled over and was now lying on her back with her legs sticking up in the air and was snoring really loudly! Lucy felt full of new, fresh and restful energy now and she felt very at peace with herself, with her thoughts and with her mind.

After some time, Lucy stood up and

gave a big stretch

She looked up at Arden and she met his beautiful wise old eyes gazing at her and she could feel the love from his warm, caring smile. He winked his beautiful wise eye at her and he gently whispered, "I am always here with you Lucy. Any time you feel anxious, lonely, nervous, sad, scared or worried, all you have to do is to use your imagination or lean against me or one of my friends anywhere and we will help you to do our 'Breathe and Root' practice. We will always help you to connect with your breath and your body, which will help you to feel calm and safe".

Arden continued by telling Lucy, "All you have to do is breathe and listen. Listen to your body as you breathe, listen to the sound of the air as you breathe in and as you breathe out. Listen to your heart beating nice and relaxed and slow. Listen to all the sounds you can hear outside of your body. Just listening, as you breathe".

Lucy's heart felt as if it could burst
with love   and
happiness   as she
stood   looking
up at Arden.   she felt
confident that   by doing the
'Breathe and Root' practice anytime,
she could help her own mind, body
and emotions to feel calm and
peaceful in any moment. She thanked
Arden for teaching her this
wonderful way of soothing her mind
and body. She gave Arden a long,
gentle hug and told him she couldn't
wait to come and 'Breathe and Root'
with him again and that she was

excited to use this new mindful practice at school tomorrow.

Just as Lucy was blowing a kiss back towards Arden and as she headed towards her house, two beautiful horses, one white and one brown trotted by on the lane at their house. Lucy loved the sound of

the horse's hooves as they clinked and clanked on the ground. But Tilly and Sam loved them even more and they darted across the garden and raced along the fence barking at the horses. Lucy called back to Arden, "Thank you Arden, see you again soon" as she raced across her garden chasing after Tilly and Sam. Arden called back to her, "You are welcome, Lucy, see you soon" and then he let out a big kind, caring, happy sigh of relief as he watched Lucy in her fun filled chase with Tilly, Sam and the horses.

Chapter 4

A Magical Mindful Adventure

Lucy was jumping with joy and broke into a row of cartwheels on the grass as she thought about her favourite tree in her garden coming to life and giving

her this very special message,
something that she could do for
herself anytime and anywhere. She
was so excited to tell her mum, dad
and Jack and to show them how to
do the 'Breathe and Root' practice.

She bounded in through the back
door of their house and

**screamed with
excitement**

as she told her family about her
magical, mindful adventure. When she
told her mum about her special
nature friend Arden, her mum jumped
up from where she was sitting in the
old armchair by the fire and squealed

with joy. She shrieked from the top of her lungs, "I knew it, Lucy! I knew that all our trees, plants and flowers are alive and they all have a special message of their own". Lucy's mum suddenly bolted out the back door

and ran across the garden to Arden. She jumped towards his trunk, wrapped her arms and legs around him and gave him a big hug and kiss.

Jack was also dashing towards Arden, shouting "Woohoo, we are going to have so much fun, Arden.

or waiiit+++++ a minute!

Were you messing with me and did you move your branches apart when I fell down in front of Lucy? Was that you I heard giggling? Did you push me out? I have a feeling that we are going to get up to so much mischief together, Arden!" Jack took a run towards Arden and he was moving so fast that he managed to run a few

feet up against Arden's trunk and he
leaped high into the air and caught
hold of one of Arden's branches. He
swung freely with so much
excitement and happiness flowing
through his whole body.

All of a sudden, Lucy's dad came
stumbling across the garden. He
couldn't find his shoes when he was
coming outside so he slipped on
Lucy's pink fluffy slippers. He was
unsteady as he tried to walk, as half
of his large feet were hanging out
over the top of her slippers. When
he finally made it over to them, he
was scratching his untidy hair and he

said, "Why are you all screaming and hugging the tree?" Lucy, Jack and mum all looked at each other, burst out laughing and yelled back to him, "This is Arden and he is alive!!! Can't you see and hear him giggling at you wearing Lucy's pink fluffy slippers?" Dad then laughed loudly and replied "Nice to meet you Arden and by the way, I do quite love these pink fluffy slippers! Now, what are we going to cook for dinner?"

Tilly was so excited that she was running around in circles after her tail! Sam was a little confused about everything and he decided that it

would be better fun to chase Tinkerbelle and she darted up into Arden's branches. Even Penny joined in the celebrations with a snort and a grunt!

The next morning Lucy got up earlier than usual to get ready for school. She made time to run out to Arden and to tell him that she was looking forward to using his 'Breathe and Root' practice during the day, when she started to feel nervous and anxious about being away from her family or about anything. Arden smiled at Lucy and said "I am very proud of you Lucy and I know that you will feel safe and peaceful when you picture me in your mind and do my 'Breathe and Root' practice with me. I can't wait to hear all about your day when you get home from school later on".

The day went so fast for Lucy at school. As usual, she felt herself getting scared, nervous and lonely during the day. So she remembered what Arden had said, and she put one hand on her heart and the other hand on her tummy and she began to 'Breathe and Root' herself with Arden and to Mother Earth, as she pictured Arden wrapping his loving branch arms around her. She felt so much better afterwards and she did the practice another five times during the day. The practice helped her so much that she felt the confidence to talk to some of her classmates at school and they invited her to play with them. Lucy had so much fun

skipping running laughing

and she felt so thankful to Arden
for teaching her how to connect to
her body and to breathe herself to a
feeling of harmony and protection
when she was away from her family.
Lucy could feel and see her heart
pumping and beating out of her chest
with love and happiness.

   As soon as Lucy got home from
school, she jumped out of the car
and couldn't wait to tell Arden all
about her day. Tilly and Sam were so

happy to see her that they jumped on her and

bumped

her

to

the

ground

and covered her with licks and slobber. Jack thought this was hilarious and was rolling around on the ground in howls of laughter! When Lucy finally got back up on her feet, she dashed over to Arden, threw her arms around him and gave him a massive hug and kiss. "Hi, Arden, you won't believe it, I had the most wonderful day," she told him. Lucy continued, "I felt sad, lonely and anxious a few times throughout the day and I did what you said. I pictured you in my mind and I did your 'Breathe and Root' practice. I felt so calm and connected to you and to Mother Earth. I had such a wonderful day and I even played with some of my

classmates and had so much fun." Lucy beamed as she told Arden.

Arden winked at Lucy, smiled and gave her a massive kind and caring cuddle by wrapping his branch arms around her and he said, "This is amazing, Lucy, you are incredible, and I am so proud of you. You helped yourself to feel relaxed and safe and then you enjoyed your day. I am so happy that you like my 'Breathe and Root' practice. This has filled my heart and tummy full of

love and sunshine,

thank you, Lucy".

Just as Arden was finishing hugging Lucy, Jack called over to her that Sam had found something amazing and to come quickly and have a look. So Lucy thanked Arden, blew him a kiss and ran over to where Jack and the dogs were. Sam was

playfully sniffing and jumping

around a beautiful butterfly that was sitting on one of the big rocks in their garden. It was the most beautiful colourful butterfly that they had ever seen. Lucy and Jack watched quietly as the butterfly stretched out both its wings and gently flapped them up and down. The colours were shining so brightly as they reflected off the sun.

All of a sudden, the butterfly opened its soft eyes and looked up at Lucy and Jack with a kind and

 caring smile. They both jumped backwards with delight. "Lucy did you just see that?"

whispered Jack. "Yes, I did," replied Lucy. "What do you think this butterfly is trying to tell us?" asked Jack. "I don't know," said Lucy but I

am so excited to listen and find out!".
Just then, Penny crept up behind
them and bumped their legs. She let
out a big snort and Lucy and Jack
jumped into the air. "Ah Penny, are
you looking to play?" Lucy laughed.

"Come on Penny, let's have some fun," said Jack. All of a sudden, the mysterious butterfly flapped its big wings and started to fly over towards Arden. "Wait, come back," yelled Lucy and Jack. "What did you want to tell us?" they shouted. They both looked at each other and yelled "adventure" and off they went to try and follow this mysterious butterfly. They needed to find out what special message this beautiful butterfly had for them.

The End

Acknowledgements

A warm and heartfelt 'thank you' to my husband Gerry and my children Caoimhe, Caolán and Sadhbh for all of their love, support, patience and trust! I could not have written this book without any of them. Feeling very grateful for all of their suggestions, edits and their ears for listening to me as I wrote and re-wrote this book many times!

Thank you so much Gerry for the amazing book cover design! You have an incredible talent and it is more than I ever could have imagined! You were able to take my hopes and visions and create these incredible cover designs. All of my dreams have come true, so thank you!

A special 'thank you' to my kind, caring and loving daughter and Creative Consultant Caoimhe McDonnell for all her incredible character and scene illustrations and guidance. I am truly in awe of her creative and imaginative mind, capabilities and talent! 'Thank you' my love from the bottom of my heart xxxxx

A sincere thank you to our amazing illustrator Laura Phillips. You were able to bring all of our characters and illustrations to life in the most incredible detail and creative way. Here's to many more projects together!

Thanks to Niall and Susan at Book Hub Publishing and their team for all the wonderful guidance, support, encouragement, motivation, laughs and above all for trusting in me and supporting my dream and visions! It has been an absolute pleasure!